SONG and DANCE

poems selected by

Lee Bennett Hopkins

illustrated by

Cheryl Munro Taylor

SIMON & SCHUSTER
BOOKS FOR YOUNG READERS

For Glenda and Rob
and sweet old 31 **C M T**

To Jennifer and Brian—
whose music shall ring **L B H**

SIMON & SCHUSTER ✓
BOOKS FOR YOUNG READERS

An imprint of Simon & Schuster Children's Publishing Division

1230 Avenue of the Americas, New York, New York 10020

Library of Congress Cataloging-in-Publication Data

Song and dance : poems / selected by Lee Bennett Hopkins; illustrated by Cheryl
Munro Taylor. — 1st ed. p.   cm.   Summary: A collection of poems about music and
dance by such poets as Carl Sandburg, Charlotte Zolotow, Langston Hughes, and Eve
Merriam. ISBN 0-689-80159-9 (hardcover) 1. Music—Juvenile poetry. 2. Dance—
Juvenile poetry. 3. Children's poetry, American. [1. Music—Poetry. 2. Dance—Poetry.
3. American poetry.] I. Hopkins, Lee Bennett. II. Taylor, Cheryl Munro, date, ill.
PS595.M684S66 1997 811.008'0357—dc20 95-44841 CIP AC

CONTENTS

IN MUSIC MEETING

Amid the sound,
The silent,
unsung greeting:
we sing together
and our voices
Touch,
in music meeting.

— Victoria Forrester

VILLAGE VOICES

No drums
No steel band tonight
Voices of the village
Outsinging all instruments

Like roots
Singing through tree trunks
Voices branch out
To leaves of melody

It is as if
Earth sings,
Trees sing,
Sky sings—
It is as if
In all the singing
This small island
Washed in ocean blues
Swims away

— Ashley Bryan

CELEBRATION

I shall dance tonight.
When the dusk comes crawling,
There will be dancing
        and feasting.
I shall dance with the others
        in circles,
            in leaps,
                in stomps.
Laughter and talk
        will weave into the night,
Among the fires
        of my people.
Games will be played
        And I shall be
a part of it.

— Alonzo Lopez

RAPPERS

Poems popping.

Dancing on cool-night streets.

Songs flying.

Poem people
Rapping song

Trapping dance

On long cool-night streets.

— *Chetra E. Kotzas*

WHAT IS JAZZ?

Jazz is a swoony
Syncopated beat
In through the eardrums
Out through the feet.
Rackety, coaxie,
Blast that beat
Whop it sassy

Sound it sweet
Clap, stomp, shout,
Blow surprise,
Shoot that trumpet
Till it cries
All the teardrops
In your eyes...

— Mary O'Neill

from **LINES WRITTEN FOR GENE KELLY TO DANCE TO**

Can you dance a question mark?
Can you dance an exclamation point?
Can you dance a couple of commas?
And bring it to a finish with a period?

Can you dance like the wind is pushing you?
Can you dance like you are pushing the wind?
Can you dance with slow wooden heels
   and then change to bright and singing silver heels?
Such nice feet, such good feet.

— *Carl Sandburg*

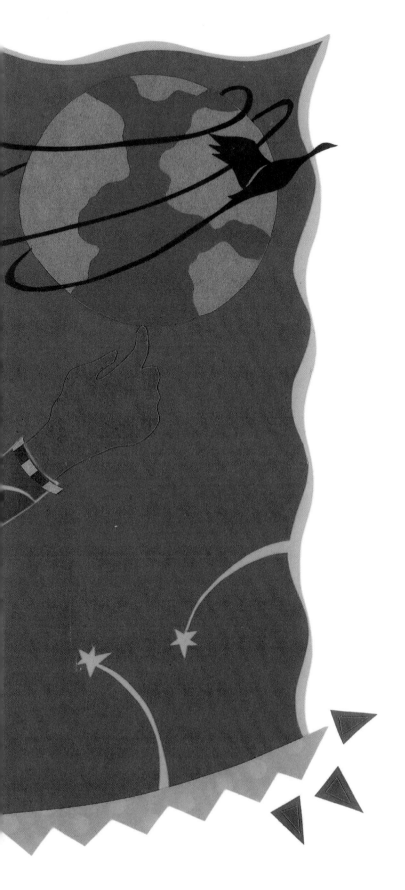

WHEN I DANCE

When I dance
caterpillars boogie
into butterflies

    wild geese disco
    lighting up
    skies

the worn-down moon
taps
till it's new

    millions of stars
    twirl
    into view

When I dance
winters
pirouette
to springs—

    When I dance
    the
    whole
    wide
    world

whirls—

and
sings.

— *Lee Bennett Hopkins*

NATURE IS A MUSIC MAKER

Nature is a music maker
whispering songs
to make feathers
dance on the wind.

Quiet as breezes
rustling grasses,
singing lullabies
to restless trees.

— Lillian M. Fisher

BIRDS' SQUARE DANCE

Swing your partner
Cockatoo
Bluefoot booby
Marabou

Cassowary
Heel and toe
Toucan, noddy
Oriole

Chachalaca
To the right
Bobolink and
Hold her tight

Kittiwake and
Tap your feet
Loon and puffin
Parakeet

Flap your feathers
Curlew, crow
Pipit, tern, and
Do-si-do.

— *Beverly McLoughland*

18

from JUNE IS A TUNE THAT JUMPS ON A STAIR

Out in the hills
where the wild hawks ride,
a bear cub stirs
by his mother's side
and waits for the sails
of the wind to rise

so he can dance
with the butterflies,
dance with the field grass,
dance with a cloud,
dance with a grasshopper,
laugh out loud.

— *Sarah Wilson*

THINGS THAT SING

Sing sing sing
crickets sing
birds sing
kettles sing
radiators sing
violins sing
leaves in trees sing
and sometimes mothers sing

sing sing sing.

— *Charlotte Zolotow*

TUCKING-IN SONG

Down the narrow hall she came,
a symphony
of jingle bells
as tiny
shiny
silver charms
waltzed like wind-chimes
on her arm,
and haunting notes
of tinkling tin
played music on
her perfumed skin...

When mama came to tuck me in.

— *Rebecca Kai Dotlich*

HARLEM NIGHT SONG

Come,
Let us roam the night together
Singing.

I love you.

Across
The Harlem roof-tops
Moon is shining.
Night sky is blue.
Stars are great drops
Of golden dew.

Down the street
A band is playing.

I love you.

Come,
Let us roam the night together
Singing.

— *Langston Hughes*

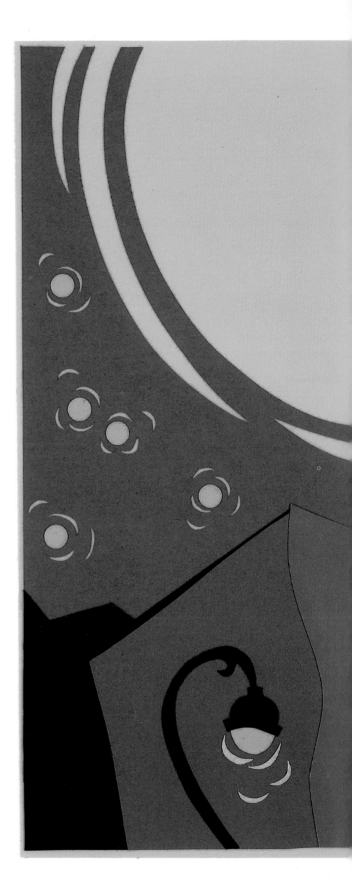

THE SONG OF THE NIGHT

I dance to the tune
of the stars and the moon.
I dance to the song of the night.

I dance to the strains
of a cricket's refrain.
I dance to the fireflies' light.

I dance to the breeze
and the whispering trees.
I dance to the meteor's flight.

I dance to the beat
of the summertime heat.
I dance to the pulse of the night.

— Leslie D. Perkins

NIGHTDANCE

All over the world
there are nightdance children;
hiding,
hopping,
never stopping,
jump rope rhyming,
late hopscotching—

happy feet
in chalky squares;
children dancing
everywhere,

and the sun comes up,
and the sun goes down,
and children moon-skip
all around,

as firebugs flicker
in the air—

There are nightdance children everywhere.

— Rebecca Kai Dotlich

DANCE

Dance out of bed,
dance on the floor,
dance down the hallway,
dance out the door.

Dance in the morning,
dance in the night,
dance till the new moon
is out of sight.

Dance all summer,
autumn and spring,
dance through the snowflakes
and don't forget to sing.

— *Eve Merriam*

ACKNOWLEDGMENTS

Thanks are due to the following for works reprinted herein:

Curtis Brown, Ltd. for "When I Dance" by Lee Bennett Hopkins. Copyright © 1997 by Lee Bennett Hopkins. Used by permission of Curtis Brown, Ltd. / Rebecca Kai Dotlich for "Nightdance" and "Tucking-In Song." Used by permission of the author, who controls all rights. / Doubleday for "Celebration" by Alonzo Lopez from **Whispering Wind** by Terry Allen. Copyright © 1972 by the Institute of American Indian Arts. Used by permission of Doubleday, a division of Bantam Doubleday Dell Publishing Group, Inc. / Lillian M. Fisher for "Nature Is a Music Maker." Used by permission of the author, who controls all rights. / Victoria Forrester for "In Music Meeting." Used by permission of the author, who controls all rights. / Harcourt Brace & Company for an excerpt from "Lines Written for Gene Kelly to Dance To" in **Wind Song**, copyright © 1960 by Carl Sandburg and renewed 1988 by Margaret Sandburg, Janet Sandburg, and Helga Sandburg Crile. Reprinted by permission of Harcourt Brace & Company. / HarperCollins Publishers for "Village Voices" from **Sing to the Sun** by Ashley Bryan. Copyright © 1992 by Ashley Bryan. Reprinted by permission of HarperCollins Publishers. / Alfred A. Knopf, Inc., for "Harlem Night Song" from **Selected Poems** by Langston Hughes. Copyright © 1926 by Alfred A. Knopf, Inc., and renewed 1954 by Langston Hughes. Reprinted by permission of the publisher. / Chetra E. Kotzas for "Rappers." Used by permission of the author, who controls all rights. / Beverly McLoughland for "Birds' Square Dance," which first appeared in **Ranger Rick** magazine, November 1988, under the title "Birds' Barn Dance," published by the National Wildlife Federation. Used by permission of the author, who controls all rights. / Leslie D. Perkins for "The Song of the Night." Used by permission of the author, who controls all rights. / Marian Reiner for "Dance" from **Higgle Wiggle** by Eve Merriam (Morrow Jr. Books). Copyright © 1994 Estate of Eve Merriam; "What Is Jazz?" from **What Is That Sound!** by Mary O'Neill. Copyright © 1966 by Mary O'Neill. Both reprinted by permission of Marian Reiner. / Simon & Schuster for a selection from **June Is a Tune That Jumps on a Stair** by Sarah Wilson. Copyright © 1992 by Sarah Wilson. Used by permission of Simon & Schuster Books for Young Readers. / Charlotte Zolotow for "Things That Sing." Used by permission of the author, who controls all rights.